Y0-BDC-847

BEAR and WOLF

by Daniel
Salmieri

Enchanted Lion Books

NEW YORK

It was a windless night and glowing snowflakes fell through the trees deep in the forest.

Bear was out walking, when she spotted something poking out from the glistening white.

At the same time, Wolf was out walking, when he spotted something poking out from the glistening white.

When Bear got closer, she could see it was a young wolf.
She could see the wolf's pointy snout, smooth gray fur, golden eyes, and wet black nose.

When Wolf got closer, he could see it was a young bear.
He could see the bear's big round head, soft black fur, deep brown eyes, and wet black nose.

"Are you lost?" asked Bear.

"No, I'm not lost. Are you?" asked Wolf.

"No, I'm not lost. I'm out for a walk to feel the cold on my face, and to enjoy the quiet of the woods when it snows. What are you doing?"

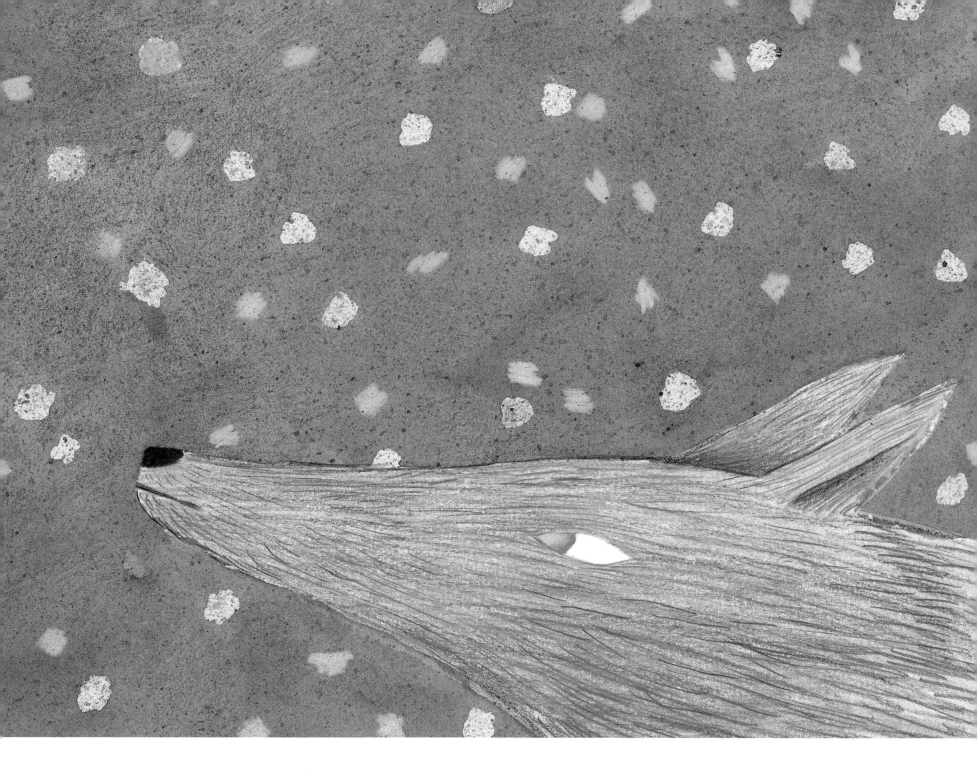

"I'm out for a walk to feel the cold under my paws, and to listen to the crunching of the snow as I walk."

"Do you want to walk with me?" asked Bear.

"Sure," said Wolf.

Bear and Wolf walked through the quietly falling snow,
using their eyes, and ears, and noses to take in the snowy woods.

They both had thick, warm fur that covered their whole bodies.
They were creatures made to be comfortable in the very cold.

Bear and Wolf smelled the wet bark of the trees and heard the small sounds the snowflakes made on their fur.

They slowed down to look closely at the different shapes.

High up above the trees, Bird was gliding through the sky, feeling the snowy air on her wings, when she saw through the branches, two shapes poking out from the glistening white.

She flapped down to rest on a branch to get a better look.
Now she could see it was a bear and a wolf walking together side by side.

Bear and Wolf continued on through the woods, looking up to notice the bird and passing quietly under the branch where she sat.

The snow was slowing as they came to a great clearing in the woods.
Both Bear and Wolf had been here before, but that was in the summertime,
when the forest was green and bursting with sounds and smells.

In the summertime, this place was a round blue lake.
Now it was a huge, flat circle of white.
They walked out onto the frozen lake and looked down.

Bear cleared away some snow with her paw.

They looked through the cloudy, frozen water
and saw fish floating, asleep in the green depths.

"I have to go now, Wolf," said Bear. "I have to go back to my cave and sleep through the rest of the winter with my family."

"I have to go now also," said Wolf. "I have to go back to my pack. We are following the scent of caribou and have many nights of running ahead of us."

"I really liked walking with you," said Bear.

"I really liked walking with you too," said Wolf. "I hope that we'll meet again."

And they turned from each other and walked away.

Bear spent the winter deep in a cave with her family,
sleeping dreamlessly in her thick warm fur.

And Wolf spent his winter running silently with his pack, looking for the caribou.

Some time passed and winter faded from their part of the earth.

The snow melted, the grass and leaves grew again, and birds sang in the tops of trees.
The forest was bursting with sounds and smells.

Bear was out walking through the deep grass,
when she spotted something poking out from the swaying green.

Bear and Wolf walked through the gentle breeze, using their eyes,
and ears, and noses to take in the awakening woods.

www.enchantedlion.com
First edition, published in 2018 by Enchanted Lion Books,
67 West Street, 403, Brooklyn, NY 11222

Text & illustrations copyright © 2018 by Dan Salmieri
Design & layout: Jonathan Yamakami

ISBN 978-1-59270-310-4

Printed in June 2020 by CG Book Printers, North Mankato, Minnesota
Second Printing